Richard Scarry's
The Gingerbread Man

A GOLDEN BOOK • NEW YORK

WESTERN PUBLISHING COMPANY, Inc., Racine, Wisconsin 53404

Copyright © 1975, by Richard Scarry. All rights reserved. Originally published in Richard Scarry's Animal Nursery Tales. Printed in the U.S.A. by Western Publishing Company, Inc. No part of this book may be reproduced or copied in any form without written permission from the publisher. GOLDEN®, GOLDEN & DESIGN®, A FIRST LITTLE GOLDEN BOOK®, FIRST LITTLE GOLDEN BOOK®, LITTLE GOLDEN BOOKS®, and A GOLDEN BOOK® are trademarks of Western Publishing Company, Inc. Library of Congress Catalog Card Number: 81-80819 ISBN 0-307-10108-8 ISBN 0-307-68108-4 (lib. bdg.)

MCMXCI

Once upon a time a little old woman and a little old man lived in a little old house.

One day the little old woman decided
to make a gingerbread man.

She cut him out of dough and put him
in the oven to bake.

After a while she said to herself,
"That gingerbread man must be ready by now."
   She opened the oven door. Up jumped
the gingerbread man, and away he ran,
out the front door.

As he ran he shouted,
*"Run, run, as fast as you can.
You can't catch me,
I'm the gingerbread man!"*

The little old woman ran,
but she couldn't catch
the gingerbread man.

He ran past the little old man,
who was working in the garden.
*"Run, run, as fast as you can.
You can't catch me,
I'm the gingerbread man!"*

The little old man ran, but he
couldn't catch the gingerbread man.

The gingerbread
man ran past
a cow at the well.

"Run, run as fast as you can.
You can't catch me,
I'm the gingerbread man!"

The cow ran . . .

but she couldn't catch that gingerbread man.

He ran between
two picnicking bears.

"Run, run, as fast as you can.
You can't catch me,
I'm the gingerbread man!"

The bears jumped up and ran after him.

They ran,

and ran . . .

but they couldn't catch that gingerbread man.

Soon the gingerbread man came to a fox
lying by the side of a river. He shouted,
"Run, run, as fast as you can.
You can't catch me,
I'm the gingerbread man!
I've run away from a little old woman,
a little old man,
a cow,
and two picnicking bears,
and I can run from you, I can!"

But the sly fox just laughed and said,
"If you don't get across this river quickly,
you will surely get caught. Hop on
my tail, and I'll carry you across."

The gingerbread man saw that he had no time
to lose. He quickly hopped onto the fox's tail.

"The water's getting deep," said the fox.
"Climb up on my back so you won't get wet."
And the gingerbread man did.

"Oh!" said the fox.
"The water's even deeper!
Climb up on my head
so you won't get wet."
And the gingerbread
man did.

"It's too deep!" cried the fox.
"Climb onto my nose so you won't get wet!"

And the gingerbread man did.

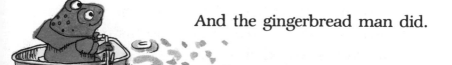

Then, with a flick of his head, the fox
tossed the gingerbread man into his mouth.
His jaws snapped shut . . .

and that was the end
of the gingerbread man!